I'd Rather Have an IGUANA

 **TALEWINDS**

A Charlesbridge Imprint

Heidi Stetson Mario

E
MAR

For Andrew

A *TALEWINDS* Book
Published by Charlesbridge Publishing
85 Main Street, Watertown, MA 02472
(617) 926-0329
www.charlesbridge.com

Library of Congress Cataloging-in-Publication Data
Mario, Heidi Stetson, 1956-
I'd rather have an iguana/Heidi Stetson Mario.
p.   cm.
"A Talewinds Book."
Summary: When her mom brings home a new
baby, a little girl thinks she would rather have
an iguana until she starts to get to know her
baby brother.
ISBN 0-88106-357-6 (reinforced for library use)
[1. Babies—Fiction. 2. Sibling rivalry—Fiction.
3. Brothers and sisters—Fiction.] I. Title.
PZ7.M338783Id   1999
[E]—dc21   97-37049

Printed in the United States of America
10 9 8 7 6 5 4 3 2 1

The illustrations in this book were done
in colored pencil and watercolor on
Arches watercolor paper.
The display type and text type were set
in Whimsy and NIMX Jacoby.
Color separations were made by Eastern
Rainbow, Derry, New Hampshire.
Printed and bound by Worzalla Publishing
Company, Stevens Point, Wisconsin
Production supervision by Brian G. Walker
Designed by Diane M. Earley
This book was printed on recycled paper.

My mom and dad got a new baby.

They said it's my baby, too.
I'd rather have an iguana.

They said it's a boy, but it's hard to tell.

 Mom says he looks like Dad.
Dad says he looks like Winston Churchill.
Whoever he is.

I think he looks like an alien I saw
in a movie once, only not as cute.

He didn't have a name, so we had to make one up.
I thought of Wisconsin and Cornflake and Spot and
Superman and Asparagus and Christine.
Mom and Dad picked Charles.

Right now he sleeps in this basket thing in Mom and Dad's room. When he gets bigger, he's going to sleep in a crib.

My crib.

Gramma and Grampa and Aunt Grace and
Uncle Howard and Mrs. Havermeyer and
even Janice, my baby-sitter, all say,

"My, aren't you so glad to have a new little playmate?"

I say **no.**

I already have a playmate, his name
is Jason Rivera and he has a tree fort
and a swing set and a dog named
Taco and six video games and

NO BABY.

Mom used to do stuff with me all the time,
like ride bikes and go to the playground
and hunt for frogs in the swamp.

now all she does is feed the baby

and change the baby

and walk around and around and
around with the baby all day long.
All night, too.

When he goes to sleep, she takes
a nap. Dad says not to bother her.

Dad does my hair and helps me get dressed and makes my lunch.

He doesn't braid right and he puts too
much mayonnaise in the tuna fish and
celery and onions, too. Yuck.

He got me a hamster, though.

Yesterday Dad was washing the dishes
and I was coloring, and Mom yelled,

"Quick, come see!

The baby's smiling!"

and Dad ran and tripped on the rug
and broke his glasses, and then all
the baby did was throw up.

When *I* smile, everybody tells
me to quit making faces.

This morning Mom and Dad were in another
room, and I went in and looked at the baby.
He was sleeping, but he woke up. He didn't cry.

I touched his hand, and he grabbed
my finger and held it very tight.

He looked at me for a long time.
Then he smiled.

 I think he's growing up now because he looks cuter than an alien or even my hamster. He can have my crib.

And you know what? He likes iguanas, too!